Wellington's Book

By Maurice Dodd

Hamlyn

London · New York · Sydney · Toronto

2

When Wellington wakes up in the morning what's the first thing he hears?

A gronnfy snoffling.

That's right – a gronnfy snoffling, say it out loud in a deep voice while holding your nose and you'll be getting a bit near the sound Wellington hears. (Best not to do it in the middle of the Library though.)

And the first thing he sees?

Something which looks like a rag mop with three prunes stuck in it. Something which, if stared at long enough, begins to look like a hairy face. Two small prunes for the eyes and a very large plump prune for the nose.

Guessed what it is?

It's Old Boot, Wellington's friend and companion, an old English sheepdog (sort of). Wellington wakes to the sight and sound of Old Boot snoring.

Mind you, and to be fair, it's Boot who sometimes wakes first and he says Wellington snores like two camels fighting in a drain and looks like a lost pudding.

There's many of you would like to live the life of Wellington. He lives all alone with his big hairy dog and nobody to bother him, because he doesn't have a mother and father. Of course, not having a mum or dad means he doesn't have anybody to *do* anything for him either. Nobody to wash his clothes or cook his meals or anything like that – so maybe you wouldn't like to live like him after all.

Wellington and Boot live in an old railway station.

They just came across it one day when they were looking for a place to live. It was just standing there (railway stations have a habit of doing that – have you noticed?) looking as if somebody had lost it, and as a matter of fact somebody *had* lost it.

You see, it had started in life as a nice little country station, and then the city had kind of grown out and around it, and then grown past it, and then the government, in order to save some money, stopped trains running to it and had then sort of walked away and, well – *lost* it.

HEY, BOOT, I'VE THOUGHT OF A WAY OF SOLVIN' OUR FINANCIAL SITERATION

WAIT TILL YOU HEAR – IT'LL GHAST YOUR FLABBER

Anyway, there it was looking lost and badly in need of cheering up, so Wellington and Boot moved in.

4

That cheered it up all right.

Sometimes at night, if it's been a hot day and if the wind's in the right direction, you can hear it creaking and wheezing to itself. Laughing. Laughing *softly* mind you, not out loud, you can't have stations staggering about gasping great gusts of laughter. Well – it wouldn't do would it?

At one time Wellington tried to turn his station into a Stately Home – I'll tell you about it.

It all started because Wellington needed money. What you have to remember is, Wellington always needs money. Stands to reason if you think about it. No mum, no dad –

no money.

Well, Wellington needed money. And he and Boot had just come back from having a holiday during which they'd spent one day visiting a Stately Home, which was a large old house standing in a stately park, surrounded by stately flowers and stately trees. Inside there were lots of stately old furniture and stately old pictures and one or two stately old people who moved now and then (the people – not the furniture and pictures) in order to take the money.

Ah – that was the thing you see. In order to look round the house one had to pay. Pay money. They wouldn't take Wellington's slightly broken old Scout badge, or his slightly bent crown-cork, not even his ever so slightly chipped very best conker. They insisted on money.

This impressed Wellington no end. Actually, first of all, before he saw how *he* could benefit from the idea, it *upset* Wellington no end.

"What cheek," he thought. "This old house is just *standing* here doing *nothing*. It's not as if it gives you any fun such as wiggling its floor or blowing air up your legs or shrieking – like the house at the fun-fair; no it stands there doing nothing. And they *charge* for it. What a swizz.

I wonder if *I* could do it?"

Well he could, and he did.

Outside the station he put up a notice which read . . .
VISIT WELLINGTON STATION, A BUILDING OF
GREAT HOSTIRIC INTEREST. ENTRANCE FREE.

It was a bit much, really.
I mean – one supposes
Wellington *could* claim it was
of *interest*, if only to himself,
but *hostiric*? I mean *historic*?
Not really.

However, he put up the
notice and told Boot to sit and
wait for the customers. "Not

much chance of that," thought Boot. "Who'd be stupid
enough to . . ?" But at that moment up came Marlon and
answered Boot's question without saying a word because
Marlon's stupid enough for anything.

As Maisie once said to him, "What kind of a fool are
you Marlon?" To which he replied, "How many kinds
are there?"

Anyway, there was Marlon, who's not very bright, and
with him was Maisie, who's not very good-tempered.

"Entrance free," read Maisie. "I'll bet – I'll bet," but

7

they both walked through the entrance to find Wellington at the other end holding out a hand which looked as if it had been specially made for the purpose of taking money.

"Entrance free – it said entrance free," complained Maisie. "And so it was," replied Wellington. "But you've come through the entrance and the rest

AN' SO IT WAS

WOT? BUT IT SAID ENTRANCE FREE

BUT YOU'VE NOW REACHED THE END OF THE ENTRANCE — 5p EACH, PLEASE

of the trip will cost you."
"I think you're practicin' a swindle on us," growled Maisie. "How dare you," said Wellington. "This isn't practice – this is the real thing."
Wellington

HERE WE ARE AT WELLIN'TON STATION — A BUILDIN' OF GREAT HOSTIRIC SIGNIFERANCE

THE GREAT ISAMBARD KINGDOM BRUNEL ONCE USED THE TOILET HERE BEFORE THE SEAT WAS BROKEN

showed them many interesting old things. There was Wellington's old chair which was years old, Boots old bone, which was months old, a very interesting spider, which was weeks old and the washing-up which hadn't been done and was two days old.

Then they were invited to visit the Wildlife Park (which was extra), and of course Maisie complained she couldn't see any wildlife.

But it wasn't for want of trying because Wellington had sent Boot ahead of them to irritate some for her.

The first exhibit had a sign saying DOG, and true enough there was Boot who does happen to be a dog. Not very interesting but quite truthful.

The next exhibit was a bit of a cheat though. DONKEY was what it said but there was Old Boot again with a pair of socks on his ears (to make them look longer), and

looking nothing like a donkey but very much like a dog with socks on his ears.

Maisie was onto it right away. That's not a donkey," shrieked she,

"it's Ole Boot with socks on his ears."

Wellington had to think fast. "I'll have to look in the official guide book," he said, dragging a scruffy little railway time-table out of his pocket and pretending to read it. "Oh – madam is quite right," cooed the crafty Wellington," Exhibit B – Ole Boot with socks on his ears."

What could Maisie say? Nothing. But Marlon said something. "We should've bought an official guide book

Maisie – then we'd have known from the start it was Ole Boot with socks on his ears." Oh he's a fool that Marlon.

The very last exhibit was THE MISSING LINK. There was no swindle about that. Not really. Well it depends on how you look at it. "I don't see any Missin' Link," said Maisie. "Of course not," explained Wellington; "it's missin'."

The day ended with an elephant ride (which was extra). "Before you go you must sample the thrill of an elephant ride," urged Wellington, wheeling out a rather sad

old elephant's-foot umbrella-stand balanced on a roller skate. Marlon clambered in and was pushed around wearing a silly grin and an empty head but Maisie was a bit put out. (Bet you'd be too by this time.) "That's not an elephant – that's only a rotten old elephant's foot," shouted Maisie. "That's true," said

Wellington, "but you see – I couldn't afford a whole elephant. Not all at once. I'm buying it by instalments."

Since he's always short of money, Wellington has to find all kinds of ways of making some, doing things which other children never have to do – and would probably be stopped doing even if they did.

One of the things he does is make buggies for sale. Buggies are sort of sports cars which look all noggley and with sticky-out wheels. Maisie always calls them boobies, but she only does it to annoy. She's like that is Maisie.

"Wellington," she says, "you're not goin' to sell my Marlon another booby."

But he usually does.

The point is, you see, Wellington is always selling another buggy to Marlon. He sells most of his buggies to Marlon, and the reason is simple. Marlon is simple.

As Maisie complains, "It's terrible the way you keep selling my Marlon your boobies. You only do it because he's easily led."

And he *is* easily led. Usually by Maisie. She's found, if she grabs him by the nose, he can be *very* easily led – as far away from Wellington's buggies as possible. She wants Marlon to save his money for things he really *needs* – such as a doll's pram and a doll's house and a doll's tea-set, *important* things, and she'll even go to the bother of playing with them to save Marlon the trouble.

She's all heart is Maisie.

But Wellington thinks Marlon was *made* for buying buggies. He can't think Marlon was made with anything else in mind. "If God didn't want me to sell buggies he wouldn't have invented Marlon," is Wellington's point of view.

One time, it was around bonfire night, Wellington

was getting a bit desperate. He hadn't made any money for some time. He hadn't sold a buggy – not even to Marlon, because Marlon's buggy was still in very good condition and he just didn't need a new one. There was little in the larder but echoes and Boot was beginning to nibble Wellington's fingers, not hard but in a *funny* sort of way, whenever they hung over the edge of the bed.

Things were so bad, Wellington even sold a buggy to himself – and then found he'd lost on the deal.

Then, suddenly, Marlon needed a new buggy.

It was all very mysterious, as Marlon explained. "It happened at the firework party," he said. "The bonfire was dying down, almost out in fact, everything felt a bit sad and the other kids were wishing we had something else to put on the fire. It was very dark. So dark you could hardly tell what was what or who was who, or even if a what really was a what and wasn't a who. Then a voice spoke to me, from the gloom. A voice mysterious, compelling . . . 'Put your buggy on the fire, Marlon,' was what it said – so I did."

You know, what was rather odd, was the way Wellington behaved when Marlon was telling his tale. He turned quite red (Something to do with the hot weather maybe, except it *was* winter), and kept shifting from foot to foot, and whistling, and found something *very* interesting to look at, up in an empty sky, and then something *quite unusual* about his everyday boots. In fact he seemed to be looking everywhere but at Marlon. I just mention it in passing.

To this day nobody has explained the mystery of the burnt buggy and the voice in the night.

But I won't go on since this story is about Wellington and the buggy he built for Marlon.

A buggy with one wheel missing.

It wasn't *meant* to be missing. Wellington makes good buggies and he worked long and hard on this one.

The body was an almost new wooden box on which the stains from the oranges hardly noticed at all. The nails he'd used had only to be straightened a bit. The steering string had come off a parcel which had been posted 'first class' and even if the pram which had donated the wheels *had* been in a stock-car race, it had come out almost

ISN'T THIS JUS' MY LUCK

FINDIN' A WHEEL MISSIN' JUS' BEFORE MARLON'S COMIN' TO VIEW THIS BUGGY undamaged.

Altogether a fine specimen of buggyhood. On the morning Marlon was due to collect it, Wellington walked around it feeling very pleased, giving it a last-minute check.

Was everything in order? Body? Yes. Roll-over bar? Yes. Steering-string? Yes. A wheel on each corner? Gulp! "ER . . . Boot," said Wellington in a trembly-lip voice, "come an' sit in front of this corner an' when Marlon comes look as if nothin's wrong, but don't move whatever you do – there's a wheel missin'."

I'm sure your ghast will not be flabbered by the news that a buggy with a missing wheel is not exactly a first-class buggy. It will tend to go in circles when it's not toppling over, which is a bit of a snag. Not quite the best buggy in the world.

And Wellington was in a bit of a fix since he'd promised Marlon the best buggy in the world.

Given a few more days, everything would have been all right. He was expecting more wheels from his suppliers, the Wheels Off Tatty Old Prams Company (which was a small boy and his cat), but he had no more in stock. And he'd not only run out of wheels, but he'd also run out of time, since he'd not only promised Marlon the best buggy

in the world, but he'd promised it for *that very day*.

He was still thinking of what to do when Marlon turned up – all sort of shiny-eyed and expectant.

Wellington did his best.

He gave Marlon a tour of the buggy, pointing out all the places of interest, and Boot played his part by sitting in front of the corner with the wheel missing,

17

looking just like a dog sitting in front of a corner trying to hide the fact of a wheel missing.

But Marlon isn't all that silly.

When he got to the bit with the missing wheel, and Wellington and Boot started shuffling about, looking as shifty as two feet in stolen shoes, Marlon began to suspect something was *up*.

"What's up?" he asked. "Up? Up where?" said Wellington, searching the sky. "What's up down there that's where," said a stern but confused Marlon. "Get away – get away from that corner . . . *there's a wheel missin'!*" He'd noticed, you see. "What?" shouted a desperate Wellington, still trying to keep it up. "Guard all the airports, seaports an' points of departure – nobody leaves the country."

It was no use. Marlon was not to be fooled. A wheel he was entitled to, and a wheel he was going

> WELLIN'TON – IF YOU THINK I'M GOIN' TO BUY A BUGGY WITH A WHEEL MISSIN' YOU'RE MISTAKEN

> IT'S ONLY 'CAUSE I'M A BIT SHORT OF WHEELS – I'LL REPLACE IT NEXT WEEK

I'M NOT TOO HAPPY WITH THAT ARRANGEMENT

LOOK—TELL YOU WHAT I'LL DO, MARLON, I'LL REPLACE IT WITH YOUR NEARSIDE WHEEL

to have.

"Tell you what I'll do," said Wellington, "I'll take a wheel off the other side and fix it on in place of the missin' wheel."

And so he did, and off went Marlon with the best-buggy-in-the-world-with-a-tendency-to-go-in-circles-when-it-wasn't-toppling-over.

On second thoughts, Marlon *is* all that silly.

It would have been all right if it weren't for Maisie.

THERE — I TRUST YOU'RE HAPPY NOW

YES

AT LEAST I WOULD BE IF I WEREN'T SO CONFUSED

In a few day's time Wellington would have given Marlon another wheel and it would have been smiles all round, but bossy-boots Maisie had to interfere. She's like that is Maisie.

"You just sit tight

20

Marlon," she ordered. "I'm going off to have a word with that Wellin'ton." And off she stomped, pushing her pram, leaving Marlon sitting in his buggy – which slowly toppled over.

Marlon did as he was told. Well – not *exactly* as he was told because when it came to it he had trouble sitting *tight*. Well how *does* one sit tight? It's another of those grown-up sayings which don't make sense. What does it *mean*? Can

you do it?

Marlon *tried* – sitting there all scrunched up like a lemon with a grudge but what with the buggy leaning to one side and everything, he gave it up and flopped out in his usual way, looking dreamy and murmuring "Vroom-vroom," which is his special

IT'S A GOOD JOB YOU'VE GOT ME TO LOOK AFTER YOUR INTERESTS, MARLON

HE SAYS YOUR WHEEL IS READY FOR COLLECTION NOW

buggy noise.

"It's a good job you've got *me* to look after your interests Marlon," said a very pleased-with-herself Maisie when she returned. "I've told that Wellington a thing or two I can tell you – and he's got a wheel for you. You can collect it now."

"Crumbs – thanks Maisie," said a grateful Marlon. "Er . . . did you know there's a wheel missin' from your pram?"

Now the fat was in the fire! And *that's* a grown-up saying which *does* make sense because fat in a fire hisses and spits and crackles and jumps about which is a very good description of what Maisie was doing.

"You – you – *Wellin'ton* you," she spluttered. "First Marlon's buggy had a wheel missin' an' now my pram's got a wheel missin' an' I'm lookin' straight at the person I think took it."

"Tell you what I'll do," he said. "This afternoon I'll put four new wheels under that pram and I'll take those three old ones off your hands – how about that?"

Maisie said "Fine" about that, and they all went off in different directions to do different

IF I GIVE YOU FOUR REPLACEMENT WHEELS WILL YOU STOP CASTIN' NASTURTIUMS?

things which is just as well because if they'd all done the same things in the same place they probably wouldn't have got them done.

ALL RIGHT ALL *RIGHT*— I KNOW YOU'VE DONE WHAT YOU SAID YOU'D DO BUT I'M *FAR* FROM SATISFIED

Later that day Maisie's little brother, Baby Grumpling, was taking his new pull-along duck for some exercise in the park. It bobbled along behind him, pulled by a piece of string. A smart-looking duck it was, painted a kind of happy yellow and had four orange wheels.

Then a strange happening took place. Certainly not the sort of happening one would expect in a park in broad daylight. An arm with a hand at the end (I agree – there's nothing strange about that) reached out from a bush. (Now that, at least, is a bit odd wouldn't you say?) And in the hand was a pair of scissors (*now* the strange bit's coming) and snip snip snip, they cut the string which was pulling the duck just as Baby Grumpling passed by!

The string carried on following Baby Grumpling but the duck . . . the *duck* was grabbed by a *second* arm and pulled into the bush!

What had happened? It's hard to say really – all *I* know is *bushes don't have arms* do they?

Even later that day a happy Wellington, with three doll's-pram-wheels in his hand was to be seen followed by a loudly complaining Maisie who was pushing a doll's-pram which had no wheels, but had a very nice line in happy yellow ducks with orange wheels tied underneath.

In the distance somebody else was following too, and catching up fast. It was Baby Grumpling who'd decided that a piece of pull-along string wasn't half as much fun as a pull-along duck.

"mi pull-along duck," he bellowed at Maisie when he caught up with the procession. (And he *can* bellow when he wants to can Baby Grumpling.) "what're you doing with mi pull-along duck?" And then he let out a bellow, which made the others sound like whispers, by packing his lungs with all the available air and pumping it out again in one great furious cry of "MUM".

"It wasn't me, it wasn't me," shouted Maisie. "It wasn't me, it wasn't me," shouted Marlon, and Wellington searched wildly for something to shout; he could hardly have shouted it wasn't him because it was.

"It's all Wellin'ton's fault," shrieked Maisie. "He

sold Marlon a buggy with a wheel missin' an' then he pinched one of my wheels to make up for the missin' wheel an' then he pinched your duck an' then he pinched my other wheels an' . . ." Just then Wellington decided what *he'd* shout.

He decided to follow Baby Grumpling's example and shouted, "Mum".

There was a sudden clap of silence. They all stood there looking at Wellington standing there with his open mouth from whence that great roaring mum had just burst forth. (No, no – I don't mean a *roaring mum* had burst forth, not a *real mum* – I mean Wellington had *roared* "Mum". Oh *never mind*.)

They were all staring at

Wellington because he hasn't got a mum. And they were all beginning to realize how desperate he must be to shout for a mum he hadn't got. I think he was just hoping a spare mum might have been passing by and would come to his aid, but there wasn't and she didn't – if you see what I mean.

"Look Wellin'ton – it's no use you shoutin' mum; you haven't got a mother," they all said. "True," said Wellington, "very true". And then as he began to sense their changing mood, the crafty thing, he began to put a lot more feeling into it. "You lot are gettin' on to me

an' I'm all alone in the world an' I haven't even got a mum."

Oh he should be on the stage that Wellington.

Well naturally they all felt sorry for him. Of course he shouldn't have done what he did, and he knew it, but *you* saw how it had all built up didn't you? And they're all very fond of Wellington really. "Hey

Wellin'ton - don't keep goin' on goin' on," soothed Maisie. "We forgive you." "Yea," said Marlon, "An' you're not alone –

you've got Ole Boot, an' he's like a mother to you."

They're right Boot," said Wellington as they both
wandered into the distance, with Wellington feeling
relieved but wanting to enjoy feeling sorry for himself a
little longer, and knowing he would soon have to start
laughing at himself instead. "You're every boy's dream of
a mother – huge an' hairy with a cold wet nose."

We hope you have enjoyed this book. Have you read the other Perishers books? There is one about Maisie, Marlon and Boot too.

Watch out for *The Perishers Very Big for its size Storybook*. It's full of amusing stories about Maisie, Marlon, Wellington and Boot. Baby Grumpling plays a few tricks too!

Don't miss *The Perishers Rainy Day Book*. There are lots of games to play and things to make. Younger children will have hours of fun with it.

Published 1979 by
The Hamlyn Publishing Group Limited
London · New York · Sydney · Toronto
Astronaut House, Feltham, Middlesex, England

ISBN 0 600 37222 7

Printed by New Interlitho, Milan, Italy